Simran Preet

First Published in February 2022

ISBN: 978-93-5472-515-9

BLUEROSE PUBLISHERS
www.bluerosepublishers.com
info@bluerosepublishers.com
+91 8882 898 898

Cover Design:
Muskan Sachdeva

Distributed by: BlueRose, Amazon, Flipkart, Shopclues

Acknowledgment

I would like to show my deepest gratitude to my parents, for their love and support throughout the journey and inspiring me to write this book for all children. I would also like to thank my publisher for helping in making my dream of publishing a book a reality and the universe for always directing toward the correct path in life.

About the author

Simran Preet, born in 1997, graduated in applied psychology Hons and now doing masters in childhood care and education. A new budding author has always been interested in fictional stories and how they can affect young minds, so combining these two interests she wrote this story hoping it'll encourage children to become the best version of themselves.

Preface

It's a story portraying how one individual can help another human being by just keeping the stereotypes and irrational beliefs. Always share your thoughts and wants with someone in authority, and maybe sharing is what needs to be heard to make other human's lives better!!!!

Story Description

Alan, a young boy staying all alone behind the jungle, one day met Jacob as he was playing with all his friends and ended up checking up the stories he's heard from the village people about the beast staying at the bank of the river. Their meeting led to a great impact on Alan's life as well as Jacob's as they found a friend in each other by..........

Once upon a time, there was a boy (living like a beast) named Alan who lived behind the forest in his cave.

One day a group of young boys was playing hide and seek in the forest and, in the evening, when they all went back home for dinner, Jacob had some other plans.

He was a curious kid which often led to a lot of incidents in the village and his heart set on solving the mystery of the beast living behind the woods. So, he took his chance today and went there. He started calling out the beast as he had heard the stories about it by the names others villagers used. After calling him out several times, Alan came to the edge of his cave to see who it was. Jacob could see him now but barely his shadow got him so scared that he ran like a cheetah.

The next day, he visited Alan again, and Alan came out covered in mud and with wild hair, a teenage boy like himself. It was hard for him to talk as he did not seem to have anyone who could help him to learn but was still able to try to speak or act out basic language by seeing other people in and around the forest doing activities like collecting wood, or children playing around but never had a chance for a real conversation with another person.

Jacob calling him out made him scared and he ran back and didn't come out the whole day and Jacob went back home. Following the next day, Jacob thought of bringing some food made by his mother to give to him. Alan went back to his cave after taking the food in a rush as he felt really hungry but also scared. This repeated for a few more days and then one day Alan decided to eat his food sitting with Jacob and started to wave at him.

They started having a conversation where Alan was not able to talk well and Jacob had a lot of energy to use and could use a friend of that same level. He realized that he is no beast but a kid who looked different but wanted to learn. After a few days, Jacob tried introducing Alan to his other friends and showed them that there wasn't a beast that lived there but a boy like us. They all went to tell the adults of the village and after all the discussion about and seeing Jacob can now have something to keep his focus on, they decided that Alan needs to join the school and should get an opportunity to have a better life but have to give a test to know which class he should join.

Before the test, Jacob and his friends tried to teach him some basics of the language and he was able to grasp it with a good speed. On the day of the test, Alan was asked to answer the questions asked by the three teachers as his friends were present there as well to support him. While the test was in action Alan was able to answer all the questions and got stuck at one where he started to get confused about the answer but Jacob and others started chanting his name as slogans with u can do it, you are doing great to encourage and support him which gave him the confidence to answer that question. Even though it was wrong, he knew that his friends were supporting him and should move on to the next question.

Alan was able to answer all the questions correctly except the one where he got stuck but laughed it later with his friends after the interview saying thank you for supporting me, helped me to gather the confidence to move forward rather than being where he was before he met all of these people. In the evening they all went playing while the decision about whether Alan was can join the school or not, and was offered a little younger class than Jacob as according to his needs. Alan was slowly able to adjust to the outer world of his cave and educate so he can make a life for himself that he dreamed of. And Jacob found a friend for his lifetime.

Moral :- Be a helping hand to someone, it has the power to change someone's life for better.

www.ingramcontent.com/pod-product-compliance
Ingram Content Group UK Ltd.
Pitfield, Milton Keynes, MK11 3LW, UK
UKHW061952290726
14090UKWH00021B/1192

9 789354 725159